Introduction by the artist

Baba Yaga is one of the main characters in the Russian folk tales of my childhood. She was almost always described as a witch, and artists have shown her like that: with wild, tangled hair, a hooked nose, and wearing a necklace of bones. She flew around in the barrel of a cannon, and ate human flesh.

But I have always dreamed of a different kind of Baba Yaga, because I see her as a powerful enchantress, mistress of the forest, of its animals and birds, and of day and night. My Baba Yaga can read thoughts, and takes many different shapes. She lives on the border between the kingdoms of the living and the dead. And while she may not always be kindly, she knows when those who are pure of heart (like Vasilisa) need her help.

I have shown her as a kind of hybrid being, half bird, half woman. But as with a shadow, her essence cannot be entirely grasped. She is beautiful and powerful, but she also inspires fear. That is my idea of Baba Yaga.

Anna Morgunova

a minedition book
Michael Neugebauer Publishing Ltd. Hong Kong

Illustrations copyright © 2015 by Anna Morgunova
Original title: **Василиса Прекрасная** *is a Russian fairy tale collected by Alexander Afanasyev*
English tex translation and retelling by Anthea Bell
Rights arranged with "minedition" Rights and Licensing AG, Zurich, Switzerland.

Michael Neugebauer Publishing Ltd., Unit 23, 7F, Kowloon Bay Industrial Centre,
15 Wang Hoi Road, Kowloon Bay, Hong Kong. e-mail: info@minedition.com
This book was printed in September 2015 by Grafisches Centrum Cuno GmbH & Co. KG, Germany .
Typesetting in Nueva by Carol Twombly
Color separation by Pixelstorm, Vienna, Austria. Printed on FSC paper.
Library of Congress Cataloging-in-Publication Data available upon request.

ISBN 978-988-8240-50-0 (US)
ISBN 978-988-8342-51-8 (GB)

10 9 8 7 6 5 4 3 2 1 First Impression

For more information please visit our website: www.minedition.com

VASILISA
THE BEAUTIFUL

A Russian Folktale retold by Anthea Bell
With Pictures by Anna Morgunova

minedition

Once upon a time there was a merchant who lived in a kingdom ruled by a Tsar, and the merchant and his wife had an only daughter. She was so pretty that she was known as Vasilisa the Beautiful.

When she was eight years old her mother fell ill, and realizing that she was near death, she called for Vasilisa, took a little doll out of the bed-sheets and said, "Vasilisa, remember what I tell you now. Take this doll, with my blessing, and don't show her to anyone else. If you are ever in trouble, give your doll something to eat and drink, ask her advice, and she will help you."

Then Vasilisa's mother kissed her and died.

The merchant mourned his wife for a while, and later, he married again. He chose a woman who had been widowed herself, and had two daughters of her own. He had expected that his new wife would be kind to his daughter, and the three girls would all be good friends, but it didn't turn out like that.

Instead, Vasilisa's stepmother and stepsisters envied and tormented the beautiful Vasilisa, who was so much lovelier than the other two girls. They sat about all day, never lifting a finger, and made Vasilisa do all the hard work about the house. And they sent her out to work in the garden in all kinds of weather, hoping to spoil her beautiful, pearly complexion.

Vasilisa bore it all without complaining. And the doll helped her, too; when Vasilisa took her out by night and gave her something nice to eat, the doll comforted her, and did all the work by magic. When day dawned, the stove was burning, the firewood brought in, and the garden weeded.

As time went by, Vasilisa grew up to be more beautiful than ever. Many young men wanted to marry her, but none of them liked her stepsisters. Her stepmother hated the beautiful girl so much that she planned a way to have her killed.

One day the merchant set out on a long journey to go to the fair, and his family knew that it would be quite a long time before he came home. They moved to a house on the outskirts of a dark, dense forest, and the fearsome witch Baba Yaga, who liked nothing better than eating human flesh, lived in the middle of that forest.

The stepmother hoped that if she found some reason to send Vasilisa into the forest, the witch would eat her up, but whatever plan the wicked woman devised, the magic doll always helped Vasilisa to get home safe and sound.

One evening in the fall, the stepmother gave all three girls different things to do. She set one of her daughters to making lace, the other to knitting stockings, and she told Vasilisa to spin flax. Then she went to bed, leaving the girls with no light to work by but a single candle.

After a while the candle sputtered and went out, as if by mistake, but it was part of the stepmother's plan. The stepsisters called to their mother. "Oh dear," they said, "now what can we do? We're still in the middle of our work."

Then they both looked at Vasilisa. "You must go into the forest and ask Baba Yaga for a light," they said. "Hurry up!"

And they pushed poor Vasilisa out.

Vasilisa went to her room and fetched her little doll, wailing, "You must help me, Dolly! I'm supposed to go to see Baba Yaga and get a light, and I'm afraid of the witch. She might shut me up in a prison—and, worse, it's said that she devours human beings, bones and all!"

"Don't worry," said the doll. "Go where they send you, but keep me with you all the time, and then Baba Yaga will do you no harm."

It was pitch dark, a strong wind was blowing, and Vasilisa was terrified. After she had been walking for some time, a horseman all in white came galloping by. He was riding a white horse with white trappings, and when he had passed, the first light of dawn showed in the sky.

Vasilisa went on and on, and after a while a horseman all in red came galloping by, riding a red-brown horse with red trappings, and when he had passed, the noonday sun was high in the sky.

At last, when it was nearly evening, Vasilisa came to the clearing where Baba Yaga lived, in a hut with a fence around it, and the fence was made of human bones and crowned by the skulls of dead men. Vasilisa stopped and stood there.

Then a third horseman came galloping by, dressed all in black, riding a black horse with black trappings. He rode over the fence, and dark night immediately fell. But the eye sockets in the skulls on top of the fence lit up so that Vasilisa could see clearly.

A rushing wind arose in the forest, and the ground seemed to shake. Baba Yaga appeared, like a strange winged creature from another world.

Still Vasilisa did not move. Where could she have gone? Baba Yaga stopped at the fence, scenting the air. "I smell the blood of a Russian soul! Who's there?" she cried.

Frightened as she was, Vasilisa stepped forward and said, "I am here, Vasilisa, and my stepsisters have sent me to ask you for a light."

Baba Yaga looked at her closely. "I know your stepsisters," she said, "but I don't give anything for no return. You can stay and work for me for a while, and if you work well I will give you the light you want. But if you don't you can never leave this place!"

Hesitantly, Vasilisa followed Baba Yaga into the house.

"I'm hungry! Bring me whatever you can find, and put it on the table." So Vasilisa did as she was told, until there was enough food and drink on the table to feed ten men or more. Baba Yaga ate and drank greedily, leaving Vasilisa herself only a crust of bread.

Before Baba Yaga went to bed, she told Vasilisa, "When I go out in the morning you must sweep the hut and the yard, wash the linen and cook the supper, and then you must separate the chaff from the wheat in the corn bin. If all that isn't done when I come home, it will be the worse for you."

Vasilisa waited until Baba Yaga began to snore, and then she took out her little doll. "Dear Dolly, what am I to do?" she asked. "If I don't do all that work, Baba Yaga will eat me up as if I were a chicken!"

"Don't be afraid, Vasilisa," said the doll. "Go to bed, and you will find that morning is wiser than evening."

When Vasilisa awoke in the morning, Baba Yaga was
up already.
The white horseman was riding by as day dawned,
and the lights in the eye sockets of the skulls went out.

Soon after that, the red horseman rode past the window, and Baba Yaga disappeared.

Vasilisa tried to remember all the work she had to do, but when she looked around the house, she saw that it was done already. The house and yard were clean, the linen had been washed, and the grain and chaff in the corn bin were neatly separated.

"Now all you have to do is prepare Baba Yaga's supper," said the doll, "and then you can rest until evening."

In the evening, when she expected Baba Yaga back, Vasilisa laid the table. The black horseman stormed past, and darkness fell over the house. The eye sockets of the skulls began to shine, the ground shook, and Baba Yaga walked in.

"Well, have you done everything I told you to do?" she asked the girl.

"Yes," said Vasilisa. "See for yourself, it's all just as you ordered!"

"Well, we'll see," growled Baba Yaga. Then she called out, "Come here, my faithful servants! Take this wheat and grind it!"

Then three pairs of hands appeared in the air and hovered away, taking the wheat with them.

Baba Yaga ate her supper and told Vasilisa, "You must do the same tasks tomorrow in the house and yard, and then you must go to the store room, open the poppy seed heads, and fill the sack you will find there with the poppy seeds. If all that isn't done when I come home, it will be the worse for you."

As soon as the witch had fallen asleep, Vasilisa asked the doll for help once more. "Never fear, lie down and sleep," said the doll. "Morning is wiser than evening, as you will see."

So next day, again, there was nothing left for Vasilisa to do but lay the table for Baba Yaga's supper. When the witch came home in the evening, she checked that everything had been done, clapped her hands again and called, "Come here, my faithful servant, take these poppy seeds and press the oil out of them."

Once again, the three pairs of hands appeared, and took away the sack of poppy seeds.

Now Baba Yaga asked for her supper. Vasilisa stood there in silence and dished up the meal she had prepared.

"Well," she said to Vasilisa, "why do you just sit there with nothing to say for yourself?"

"I hardly dare talk to you," said Vasilisa the Beautiful, "but if I did, I would certainly like to ask you some questions."

"Ask away," said the witch "but remember that not every question has a good answer, and the more you know the sooner you grow old."

"I only want to ask about some of the things I saw on my way here," said Vasilisa. "I saw three riders, one in white, one in red, and one in black. Who were they?"

"All three are my faithful servants," said Baba Yaga. "They help me to divide the day and the night. The white rider is the Dawn of Day, the red rider is the Sun at Noon, and the black rider is the Dark of Night. Is there anything else you want to know?"

Vasilisa remembered the three pairs of hands, but she decided to be on the safe side and keep her mouth shut, which was just as well.

"I'm glad that's all you wanted to ask, for I destroy all who are too inquisitive," said Baba Yaga. "Now it's my turn to ask you a question: how did you do all that work for me so quickly?"

Vasilisa decided to keep her mouth shut about the magic doll as well. "Why," said she, "my dying mother gave me her blessing, and that has always helped me."

"So that's it, is it? Off you go this minute, then," said Baba Yaga, cursing. "I don't like folk with blessings on them in this place." And she threw Vasilisa out of her house. As Vasilisa approached the fence, however, the witch took down one of the skulls with shining eyes, and placed it on the end of a pole.
"This is what you came for, isn't it?" she asked Vasilisa. "A light for your stepsisters. So take it, and be off with you."

It took Vasilisa a day and a night to find her way back, but the light from the eye sockets of the skull showed her the way through the dark forest.
When she was very close to home, she was going to throw
the skull away, but she heard it speak
in a hollow voice, saying,
"Don't throw me away.
Take me into the house."

Vasilisa saw that there was not a single light burning indoors. Her stepmother and stepsisters opened the door, and began complaining. "We haven't been able to strike a light of any kind since you left, and if we went to the neighbors for fire, it went out of its own accord as soon as it crossed our threshold. Let's hope this light of yours will stay alight."

Vasilisa carried the skull into the house. Its eyes blazed more brightly than ever, burning like fire, following her stepmother and stepsisters wherever they went. They tried to hide from the light, but it was no use.
By next morning all three of them had burned to ashes, but no harm came to Vasilisa the Beautiful at all.

Vasilisa buried the ashes and the skull in the garden, locked up the house, and set off for the nearest town. She found a place to stay with a kind old woman who lived alone, deciding to wait there for her father's return.

One day she told the old woman, "I'm used to hard work, and I get bored with nothing to do, Grandma. Please go to market, buy the best flax they have for sale, and bring it back for me to spin."

The old woman did as she asked, and with the spindle dancing in her fingers, Vasilisa spun the flax into the finest yarn ever seen, no thicker than a spider's silken cobweb. However, when she wanted to weave the thread into fabric, there was no loom that could take such fine yarn.

Once again the magic doll came to her aid, and made her a loom delicate enough to weave the thread. Vasilisa spent all winter weaving linen so fine, soft and delicate that you could pass it through a needle's eye.

In spring she bleached it in the meadows, in the warm sun and the fresh air, and she told the old woman, "Take this cloth to market, Grandma, sell it and keep the money for yourself, because you have been so kind to me."
"Oh no," said the old woman. "The cloth is too fine to sell, and too good for anyone but our young Tsar to wear. I shall take it to court for him."

She went to the royal palace and asked to see the young Tsar, saying she would show her precious wares to him alone. He called her in, admired the cloth, and asked how much it cost.
"It is beyond price," said the old woman. "No one but a Tsar like Your Majesty should wear it, and I am making you a present of it." The Tsar thanked the old woman, and gave her many valuable gifts in return. Then he asked his tailors to make him shirts from the wonderful fabric, but they said it was too delicate for their needles, and they dared not touch it.

So he sent for the old woman, and said, "Since you spun and wove this exquisite linen, I am sure you will be able to make it into shirts for me."
"Your Majesty," said the old woman, bowing, "it was not I but my foster daughter who spun the flax and wove it into this fine linen."

"Then ask your daughter to make me some shirts," said the Tsar.

The old woman went home and told Vasilisa what the Tsar had said. Vasilisa smiled and replied, "I had an idea that this would be work fit for me!" Alone in her room, with her pretty fingers flying, she made a dozen soft and delicate shirts in no time at all.

While the old woman took them to the Tsar, Vasilisa bathed, did her hair prettily, dressed in her best, and sat at the window. Soon a messenger from the young Tsar rode into the yard. He knocked on the door, and said that his master wanted to see the clever seamstress who had made such soft shirts for him, so that he could thank her in person.

So Vasilisa the Beautiful went to the palace, and when the Tsar set eyes on her, he was instantly smitten. They fell in love at once. "I cannot let you go away, my sweet and beautiful girl!" he said. "Be my wife, and we will rule the kingdom together."

They were married without delay, and when Vasilisa's father came back from his long journey he was delighted to find his daughter so well and happy, and married to the Tsar of the kingdom, too. He went to live with her and the Tsar at court, and the kind old woman was brought to live at the palace as well.

As for the magic doll that Vasilisa's mother had given her, with her blessing, the young Tsarina carried her around with her for the rest of her life.

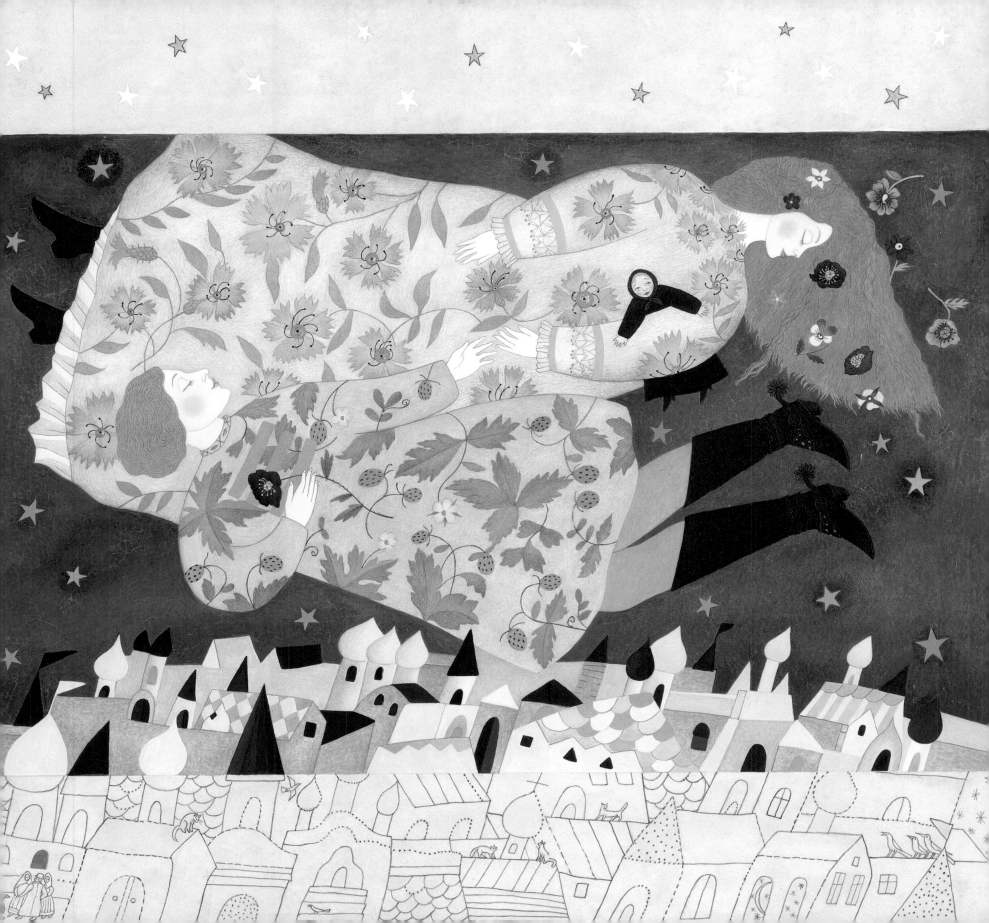